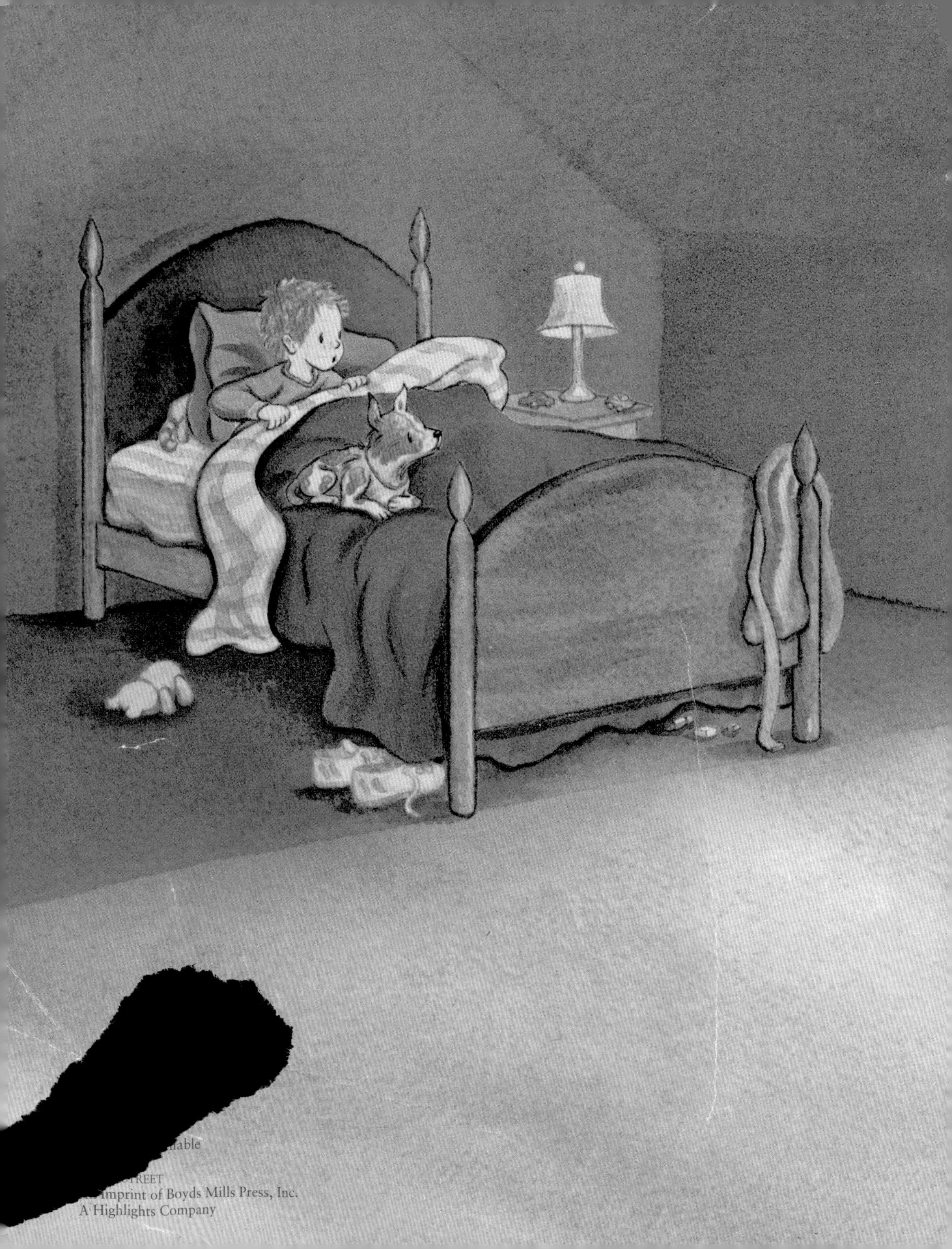

ilable

REET
Imprint of Boyds Mills Press, Inc.
A Highlights Company

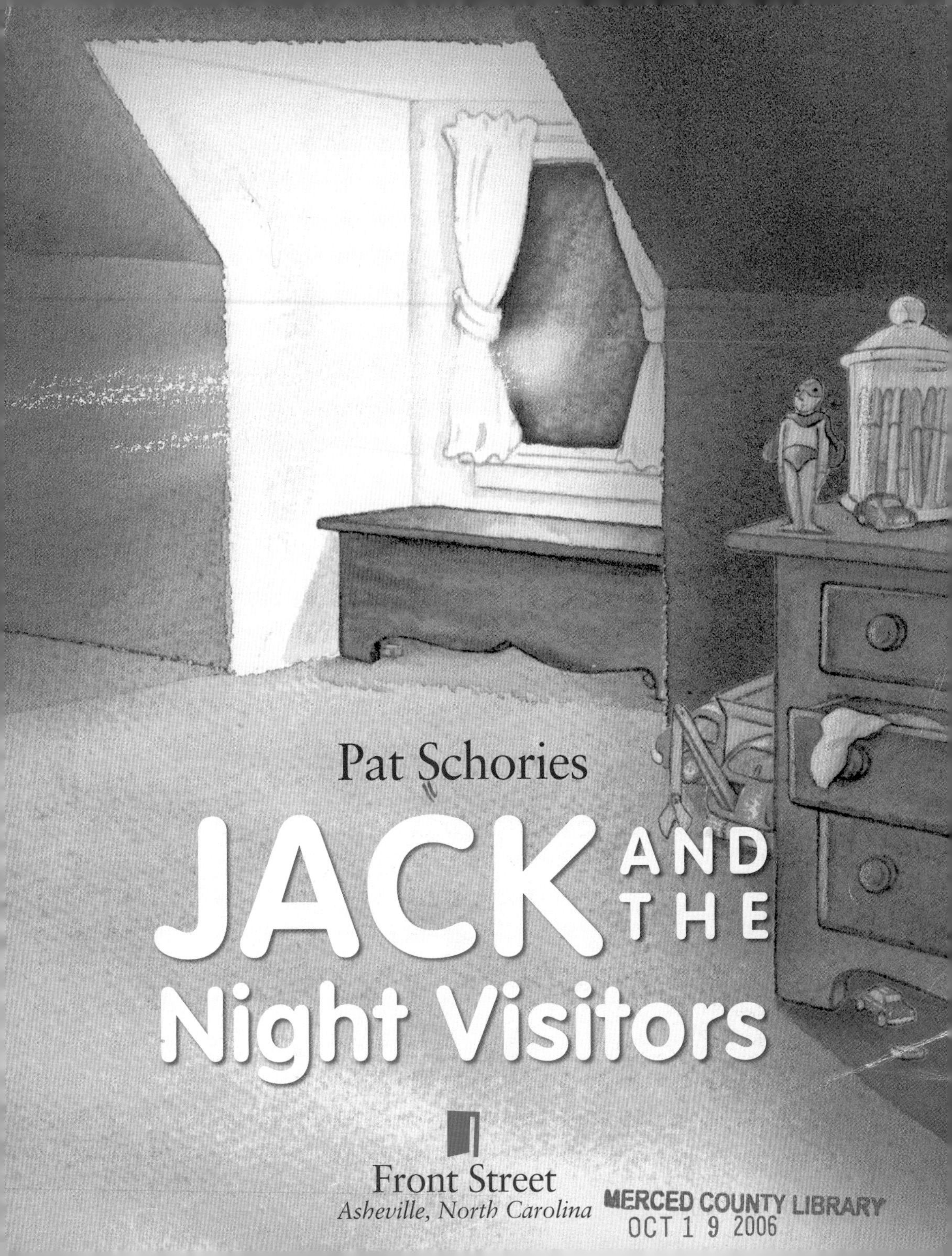

Pat Schories

JACK AND THE Night Visitors

Front Street
Asheville, North Carolina

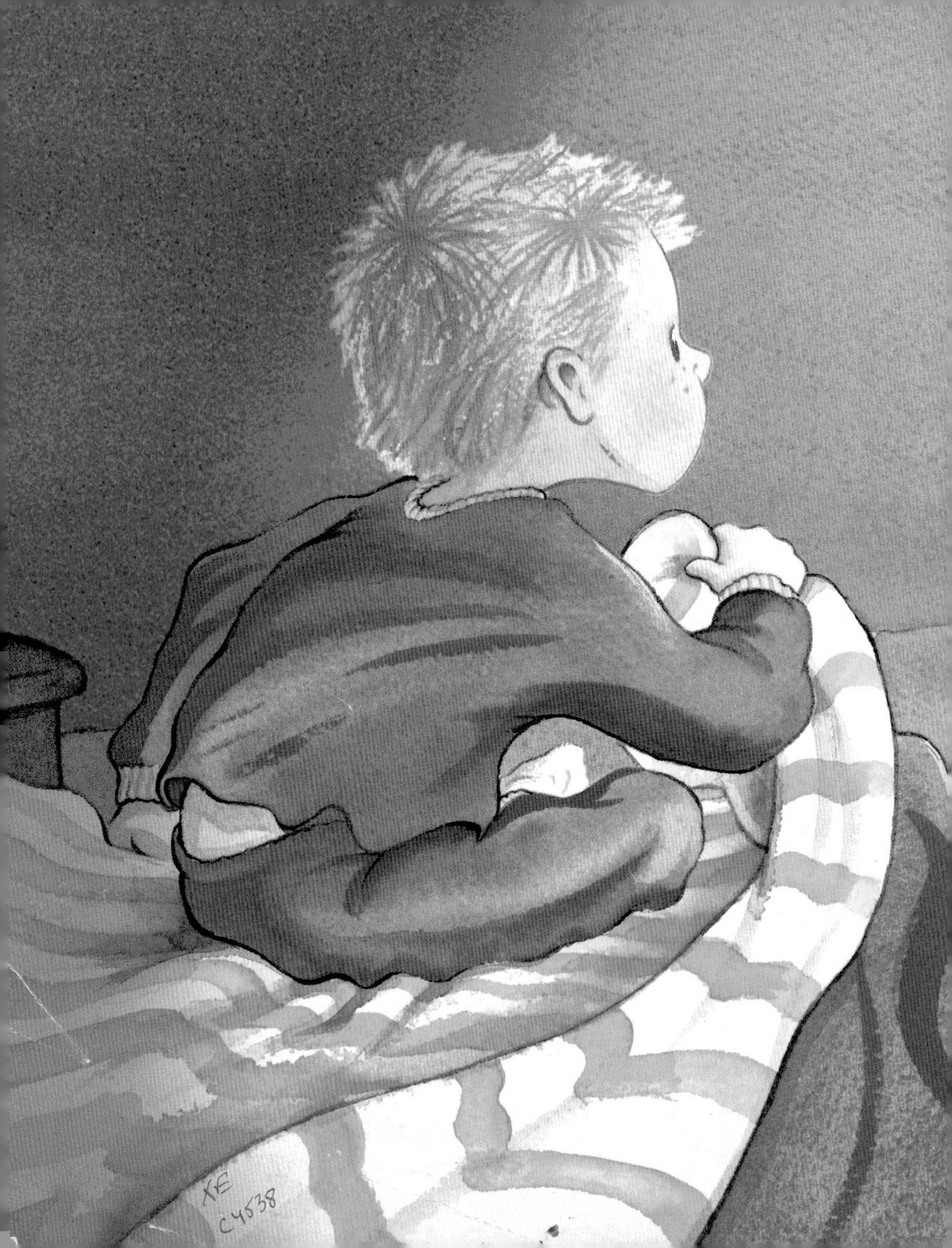

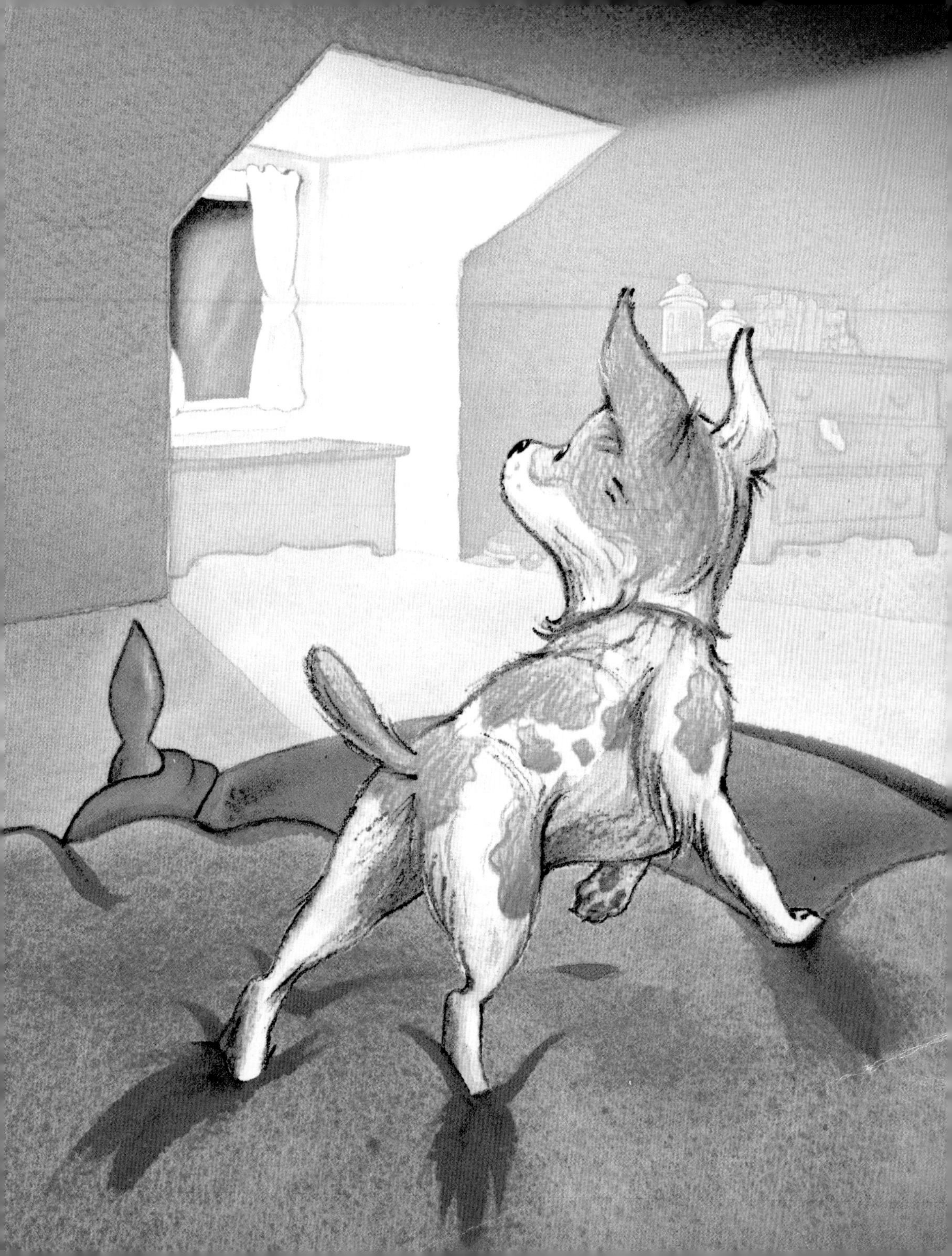

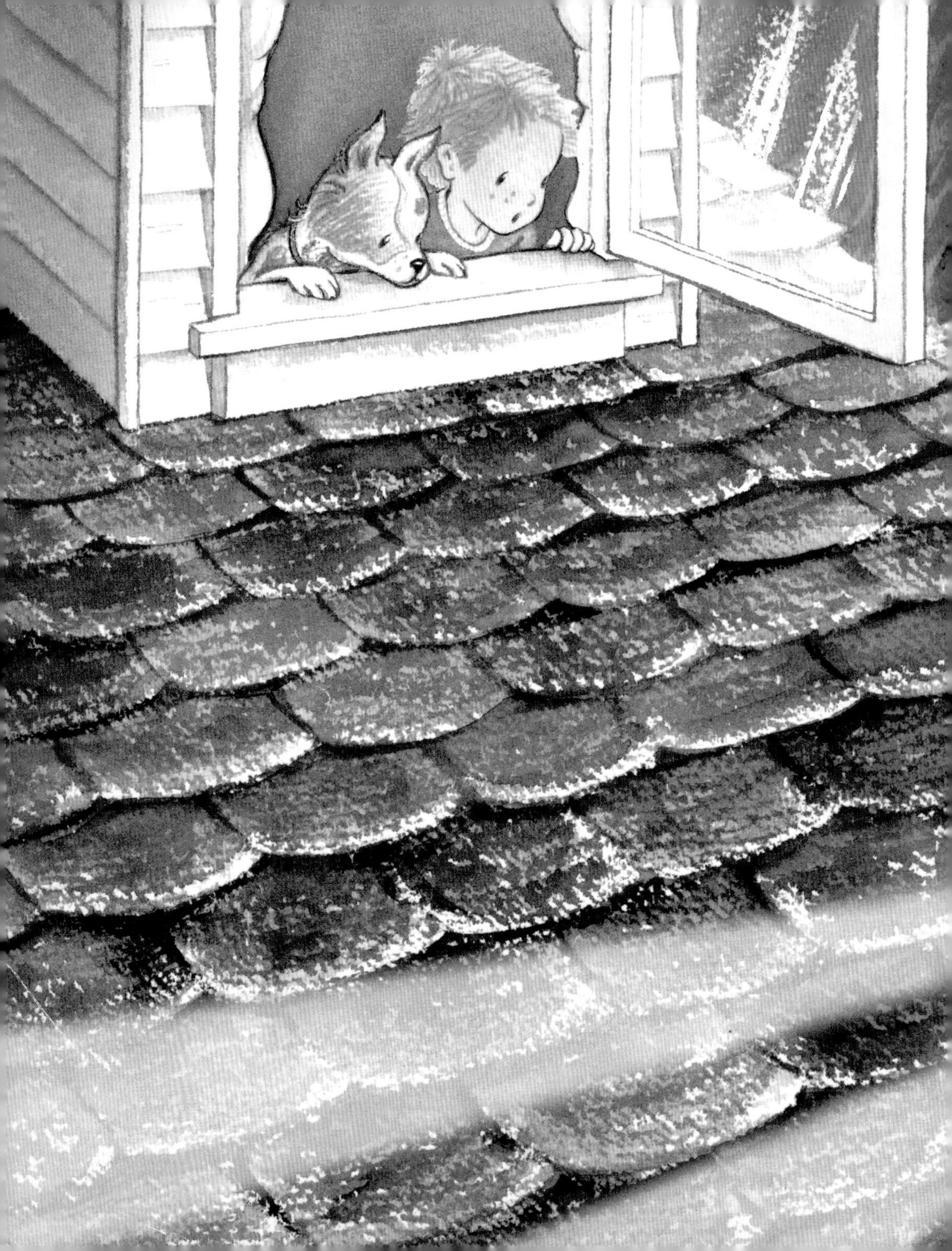

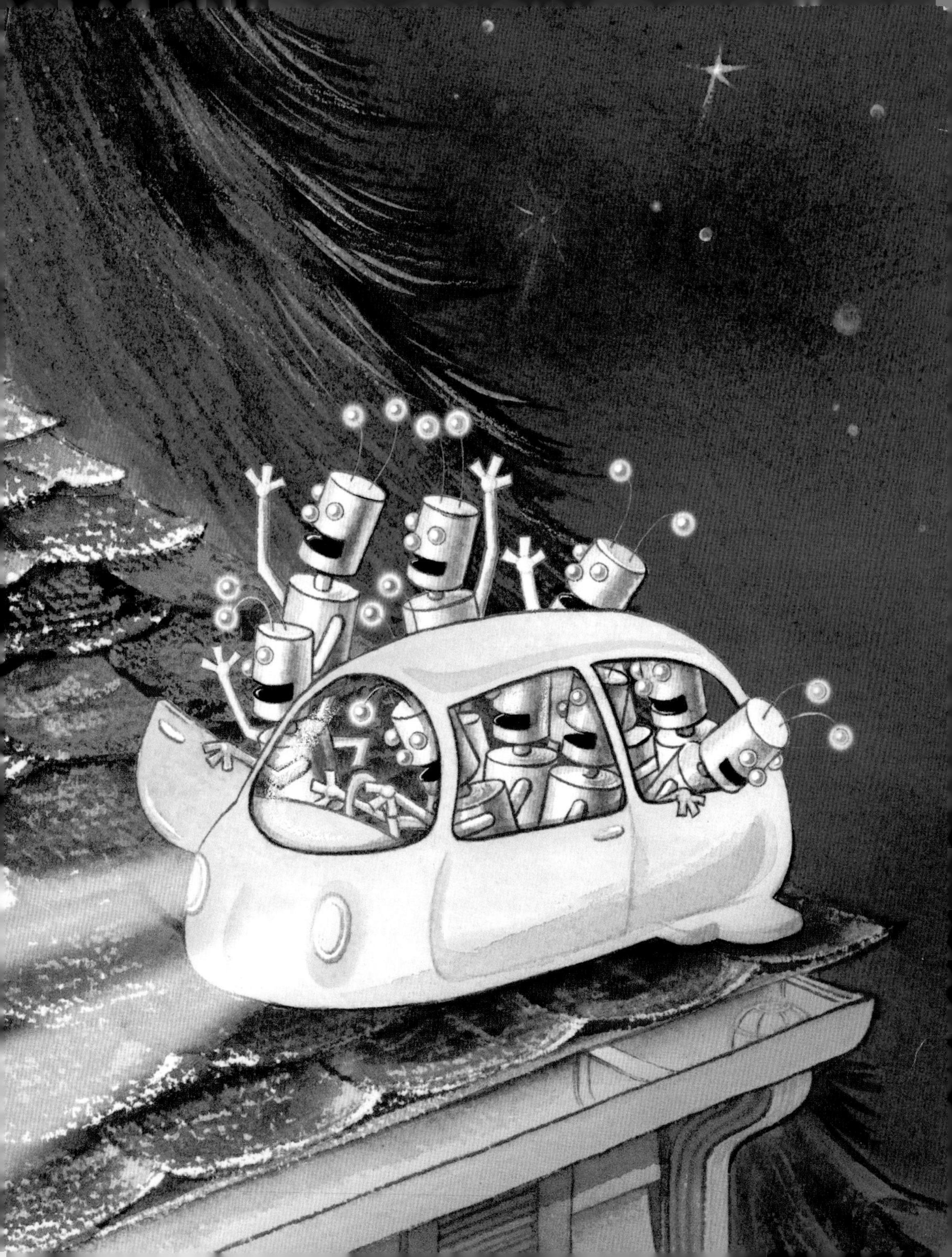

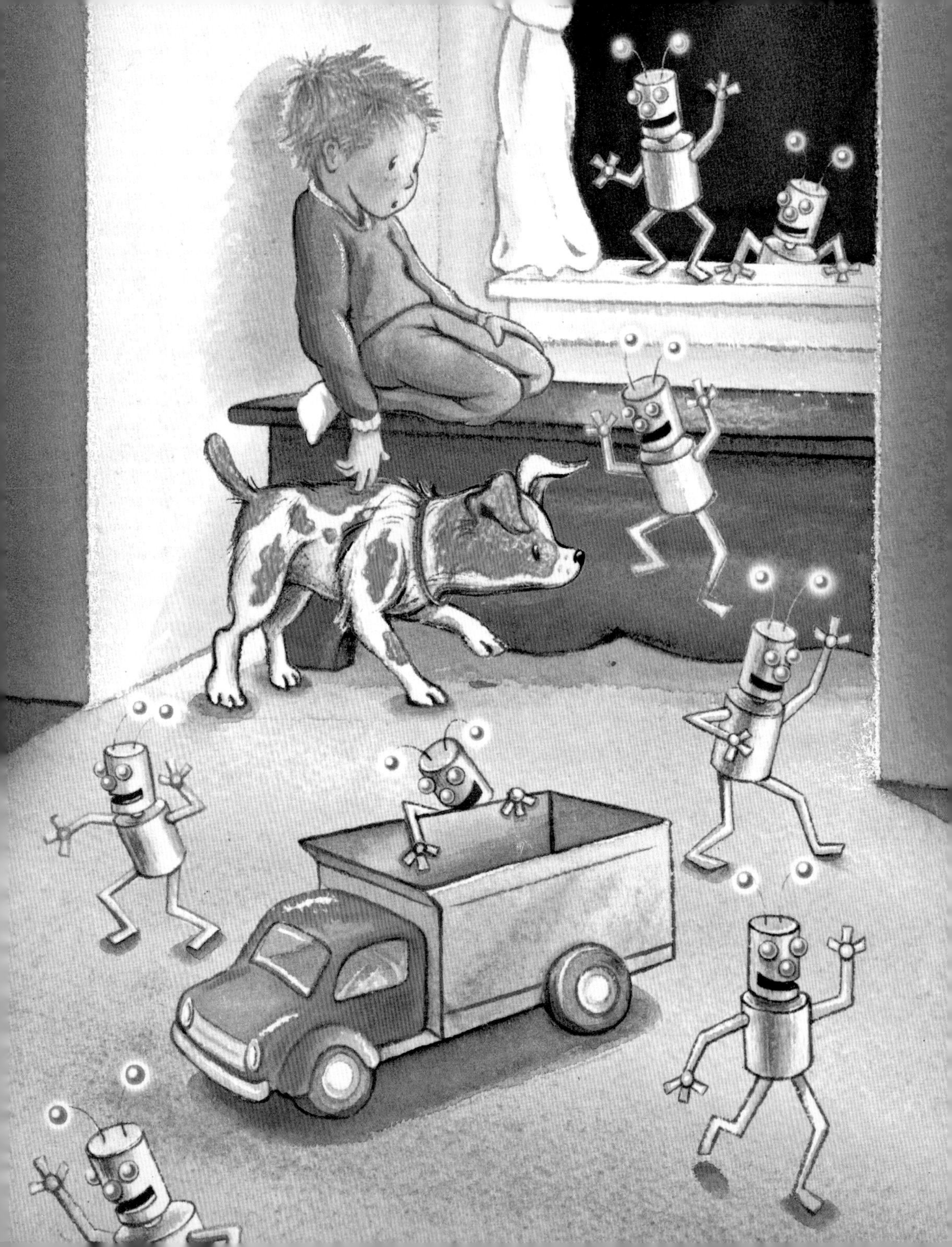

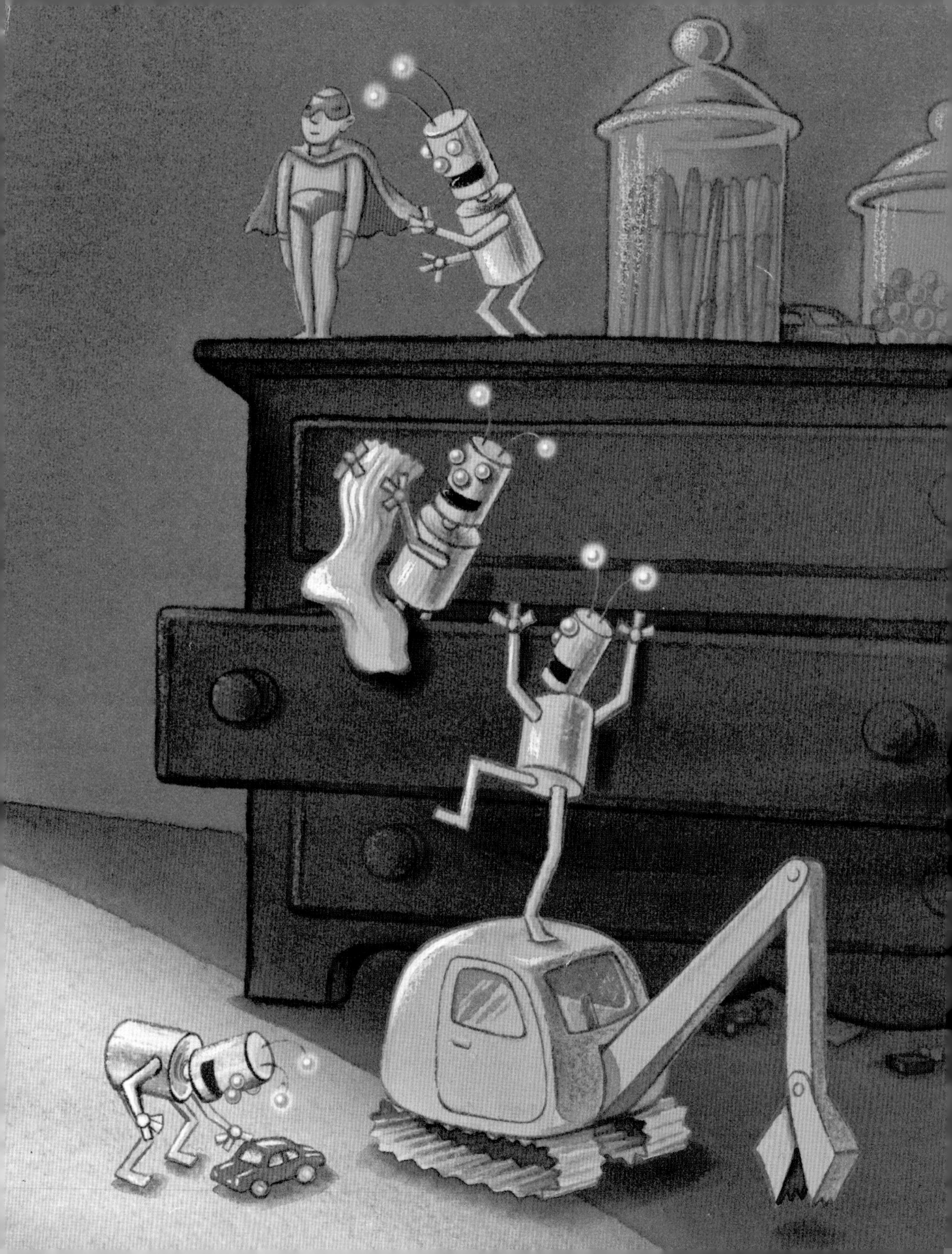

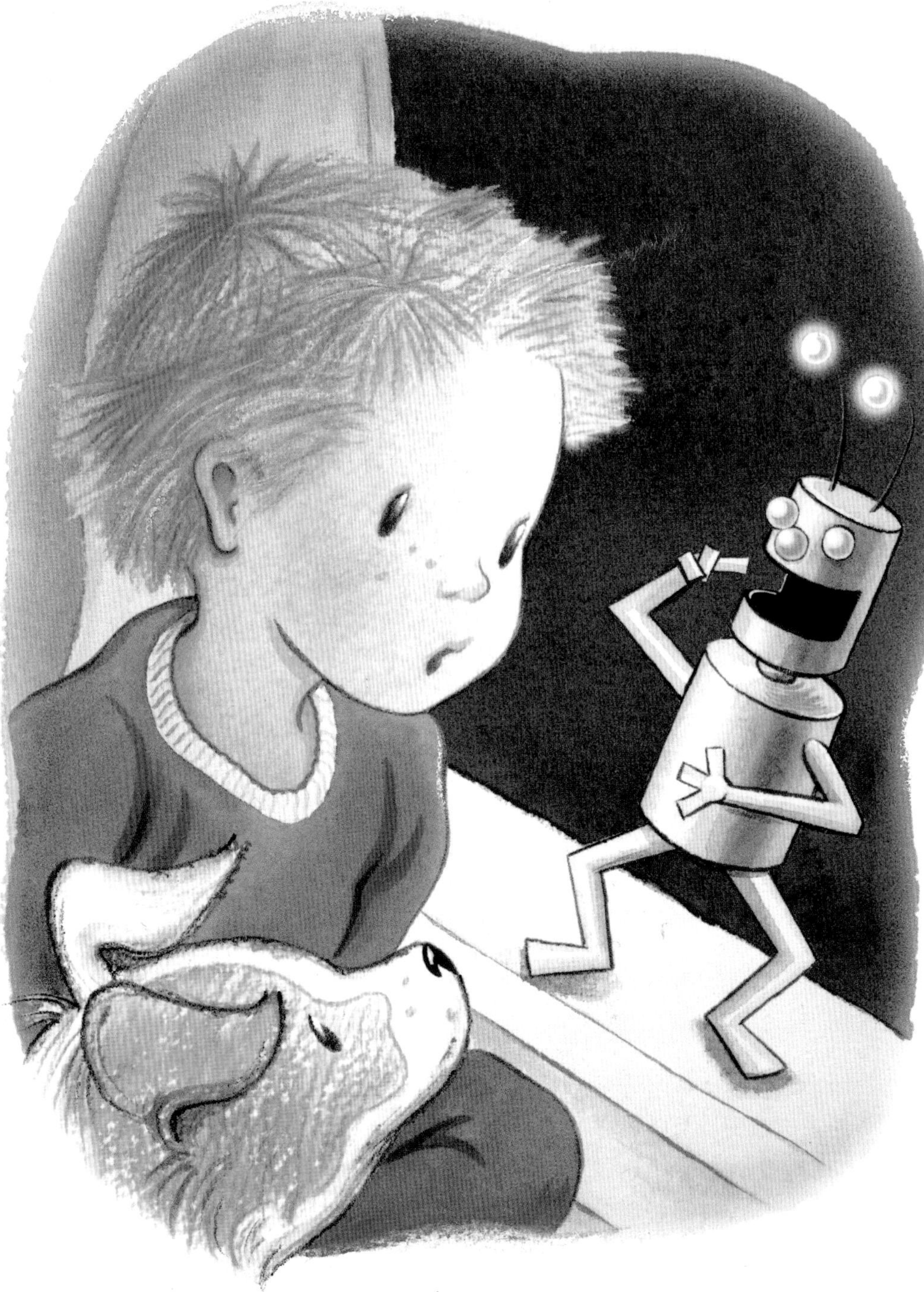

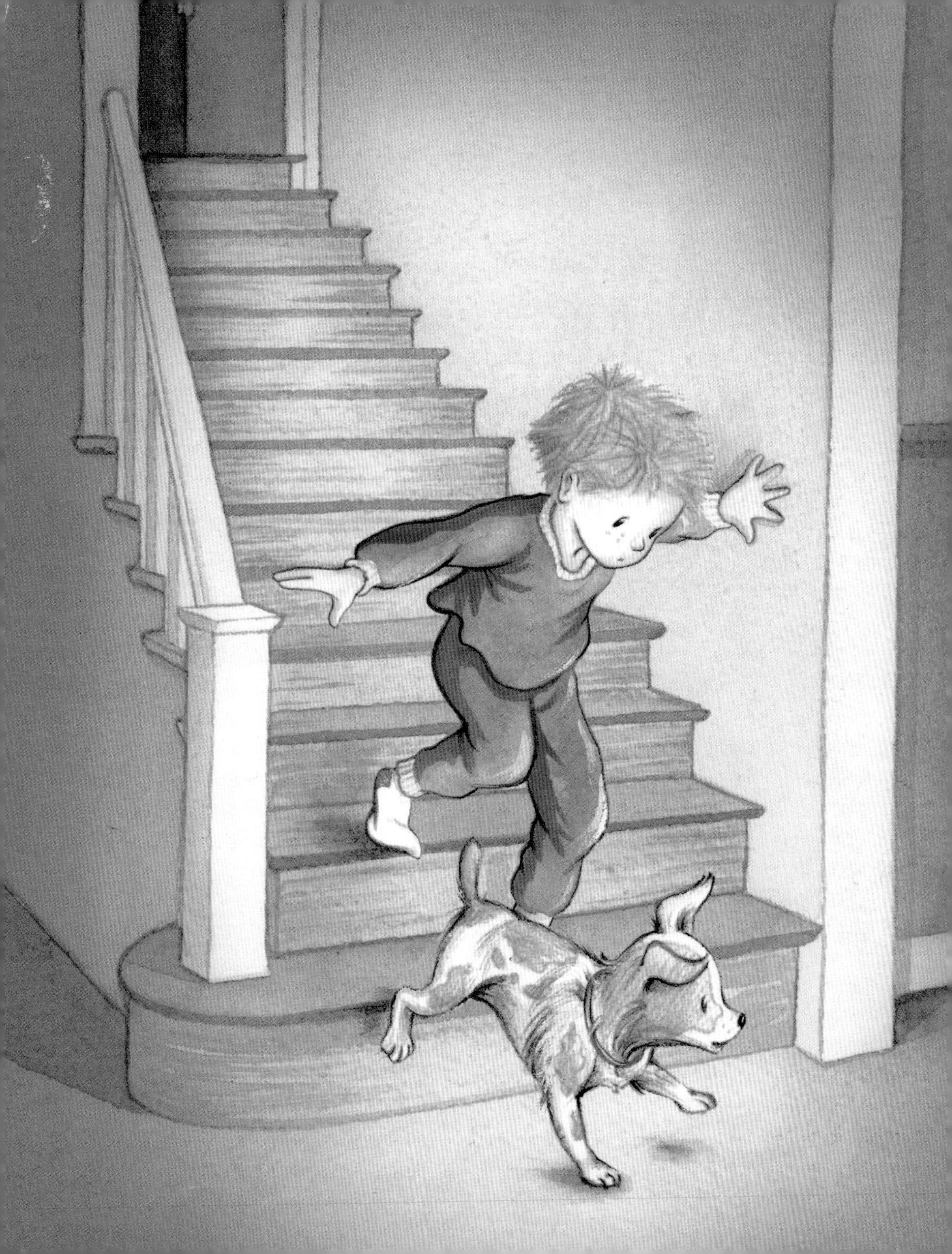

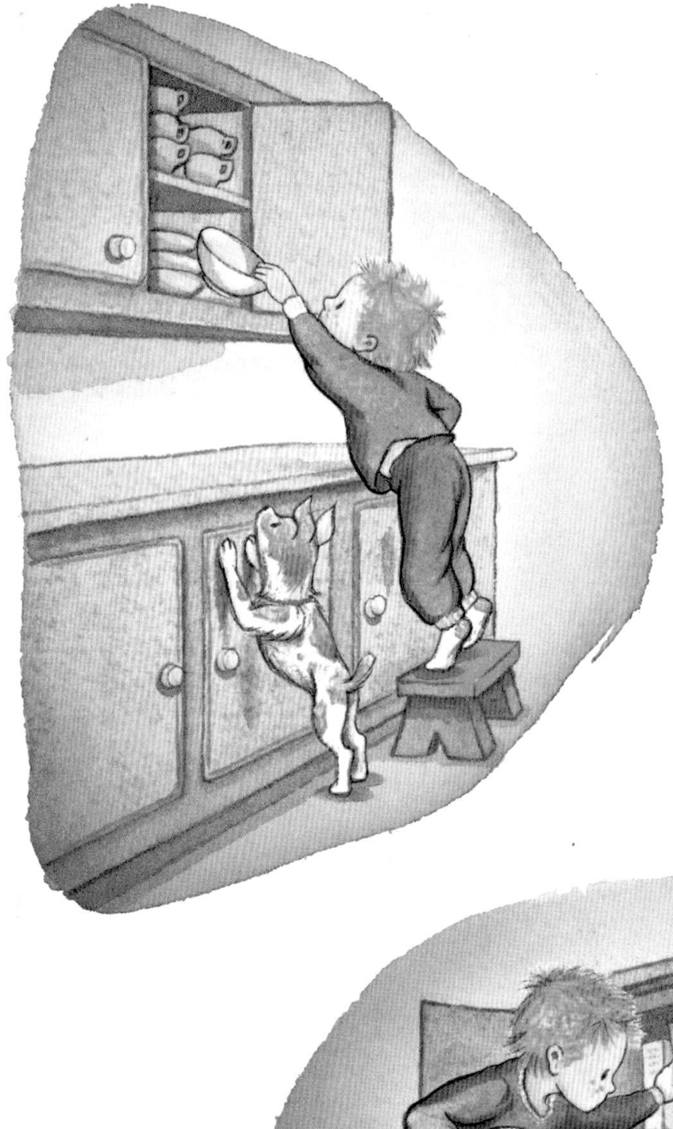

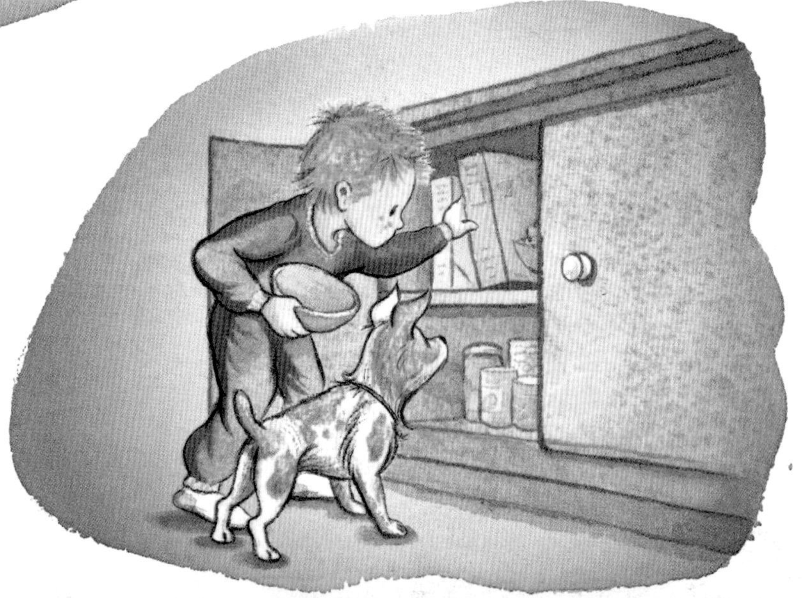

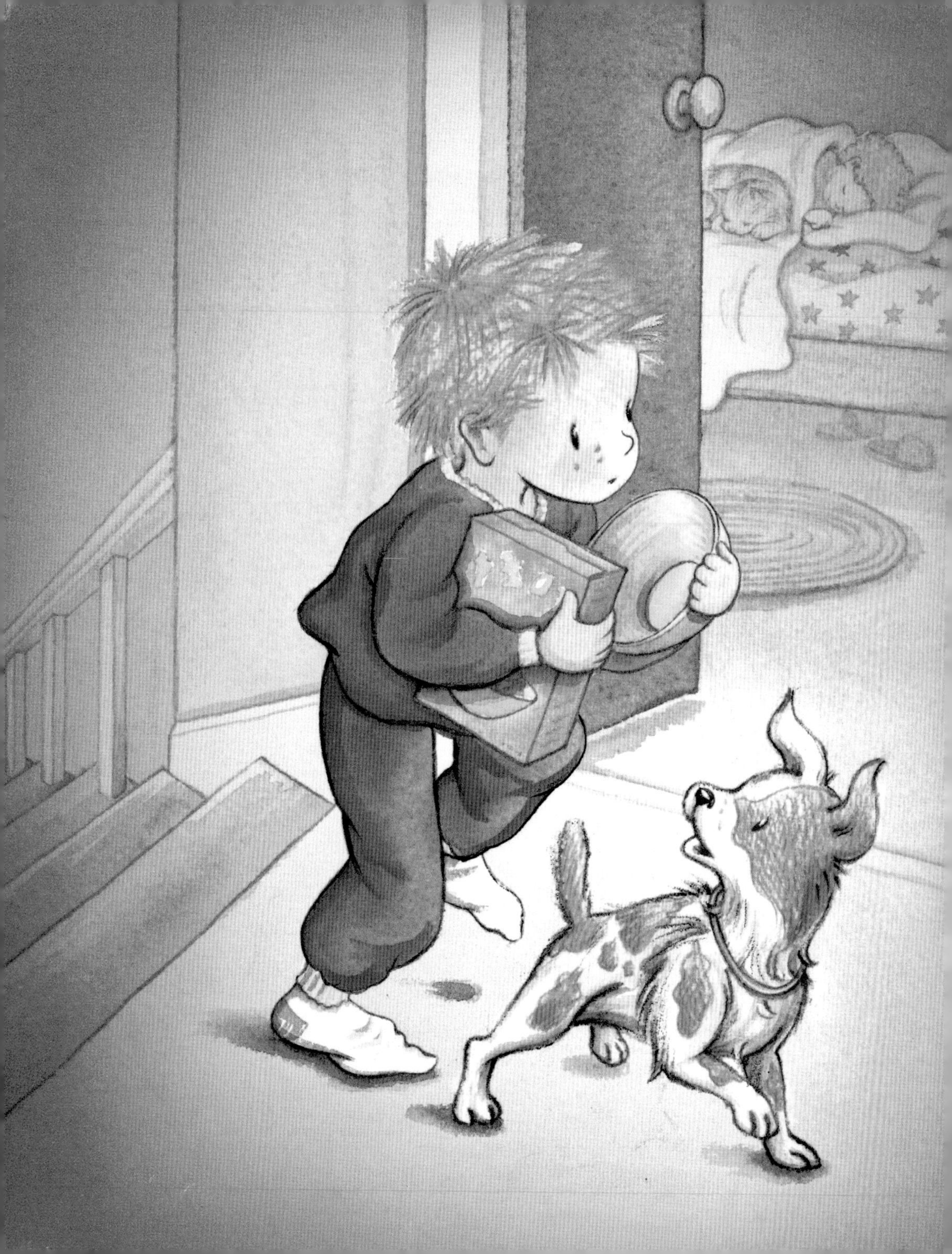

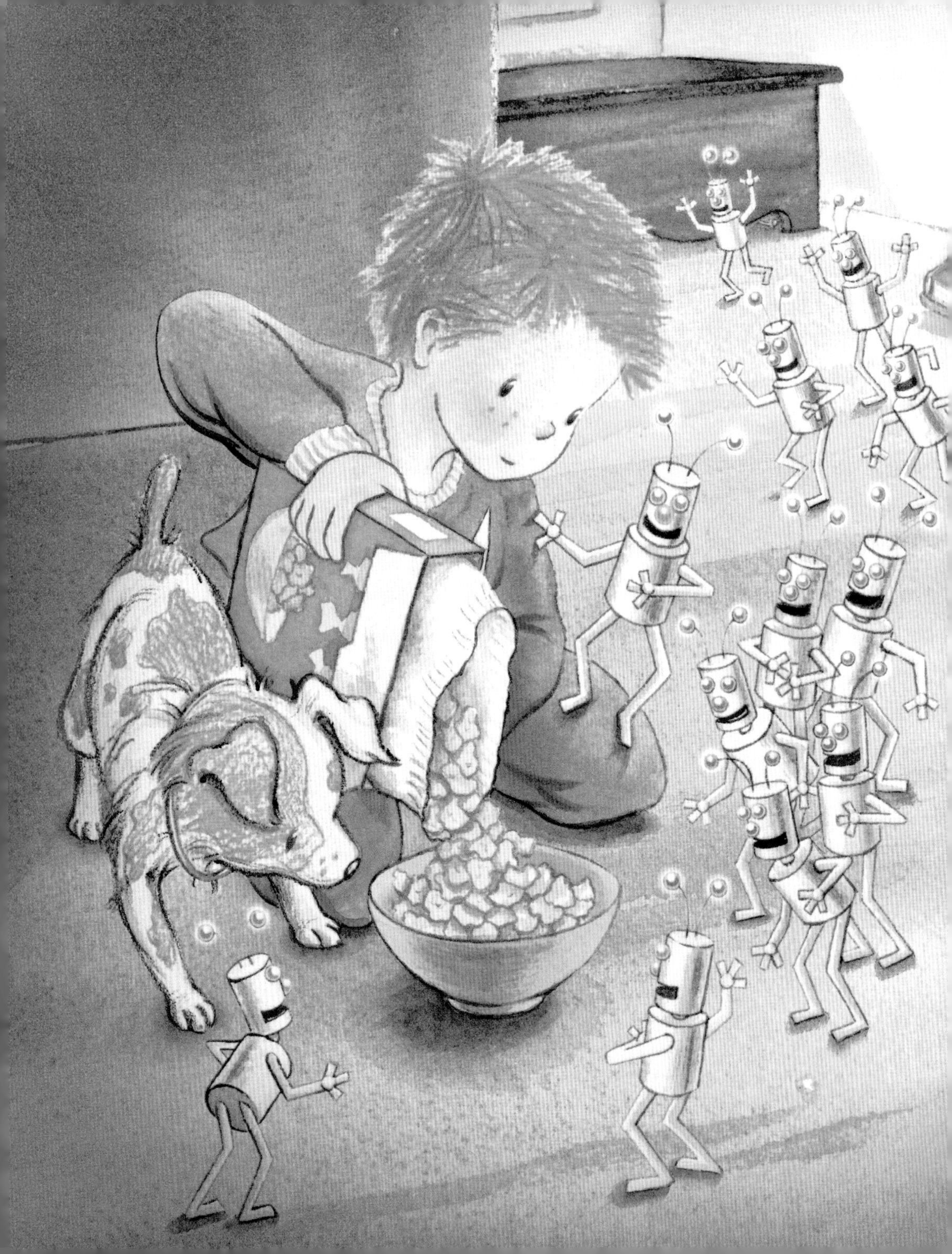

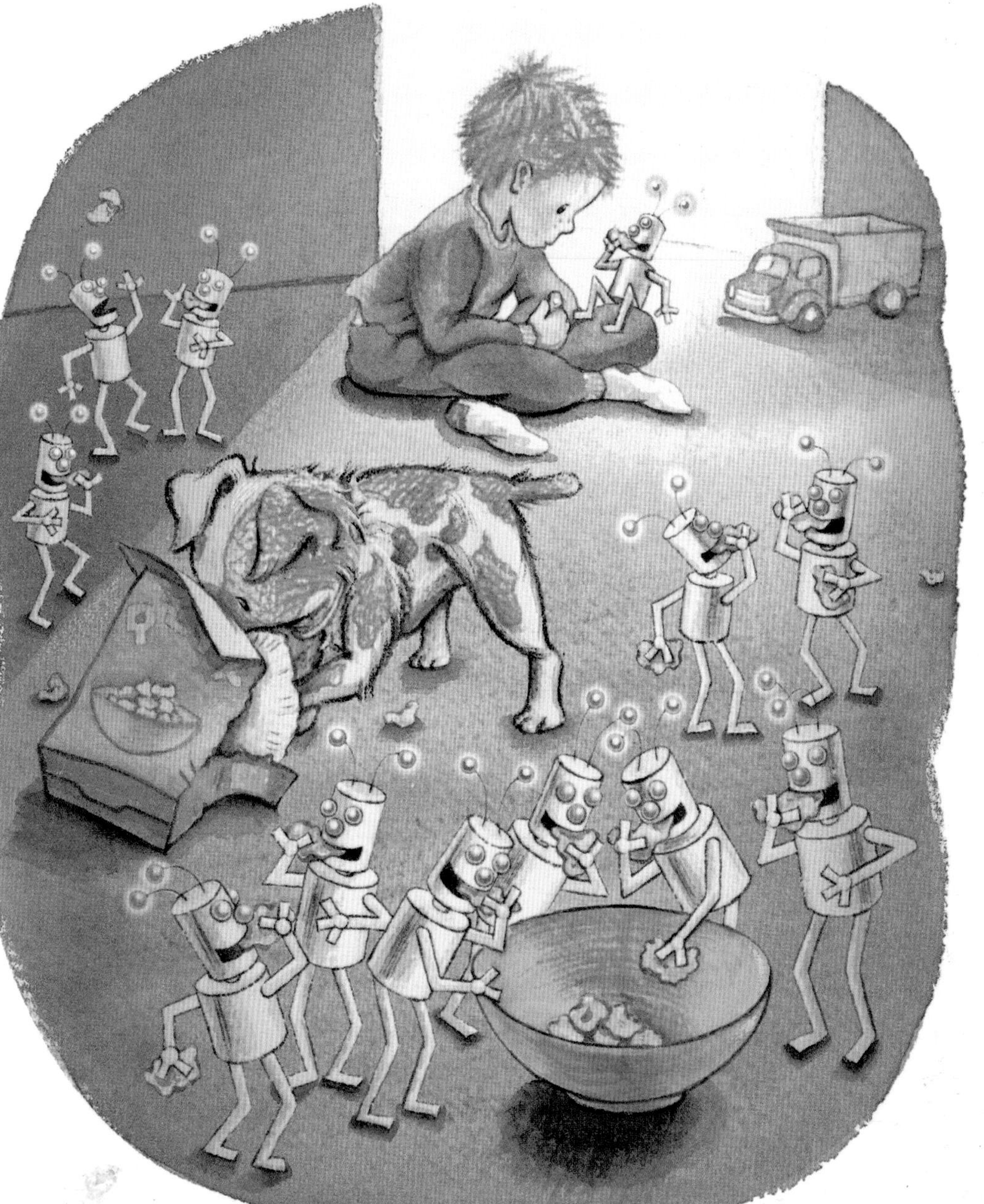

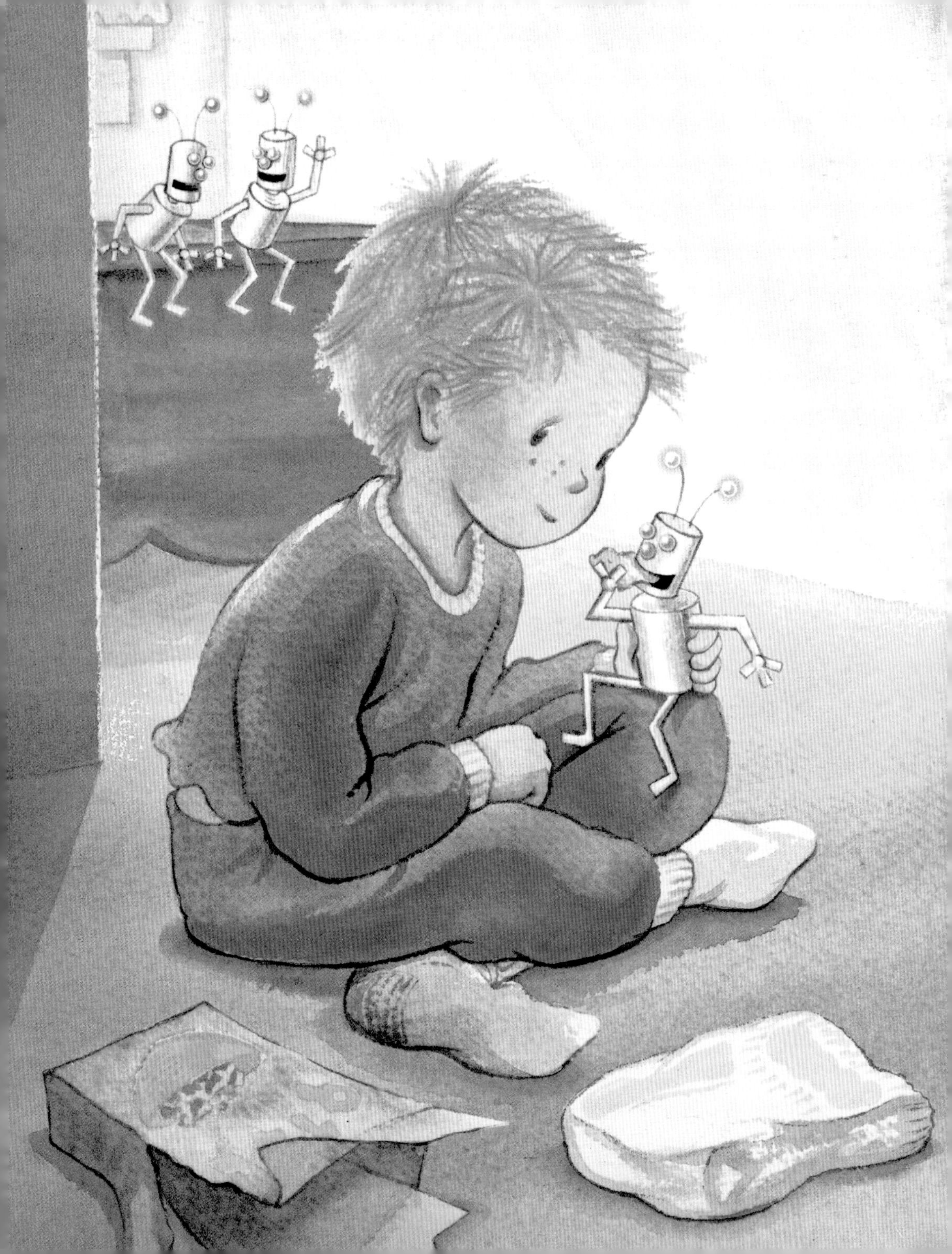

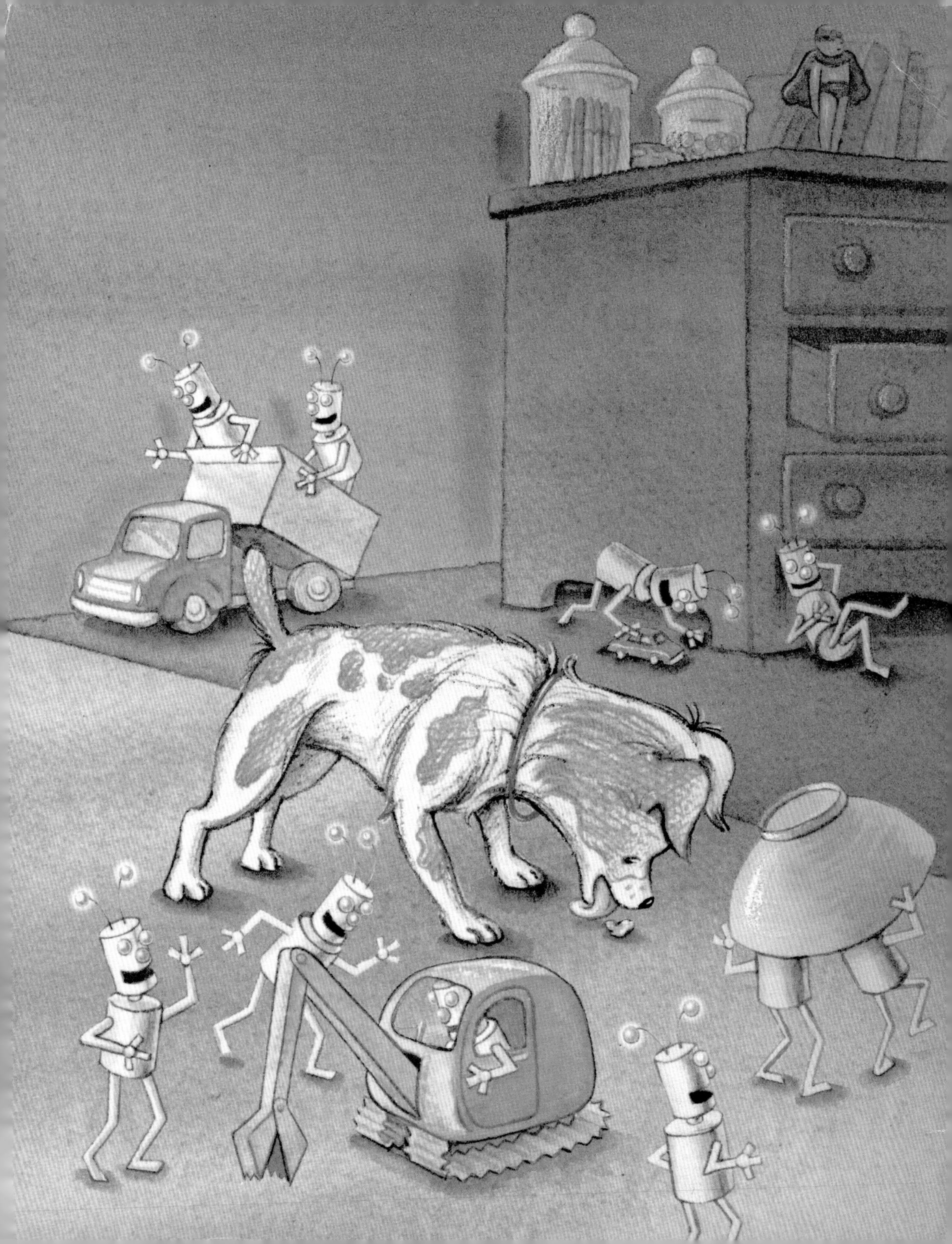

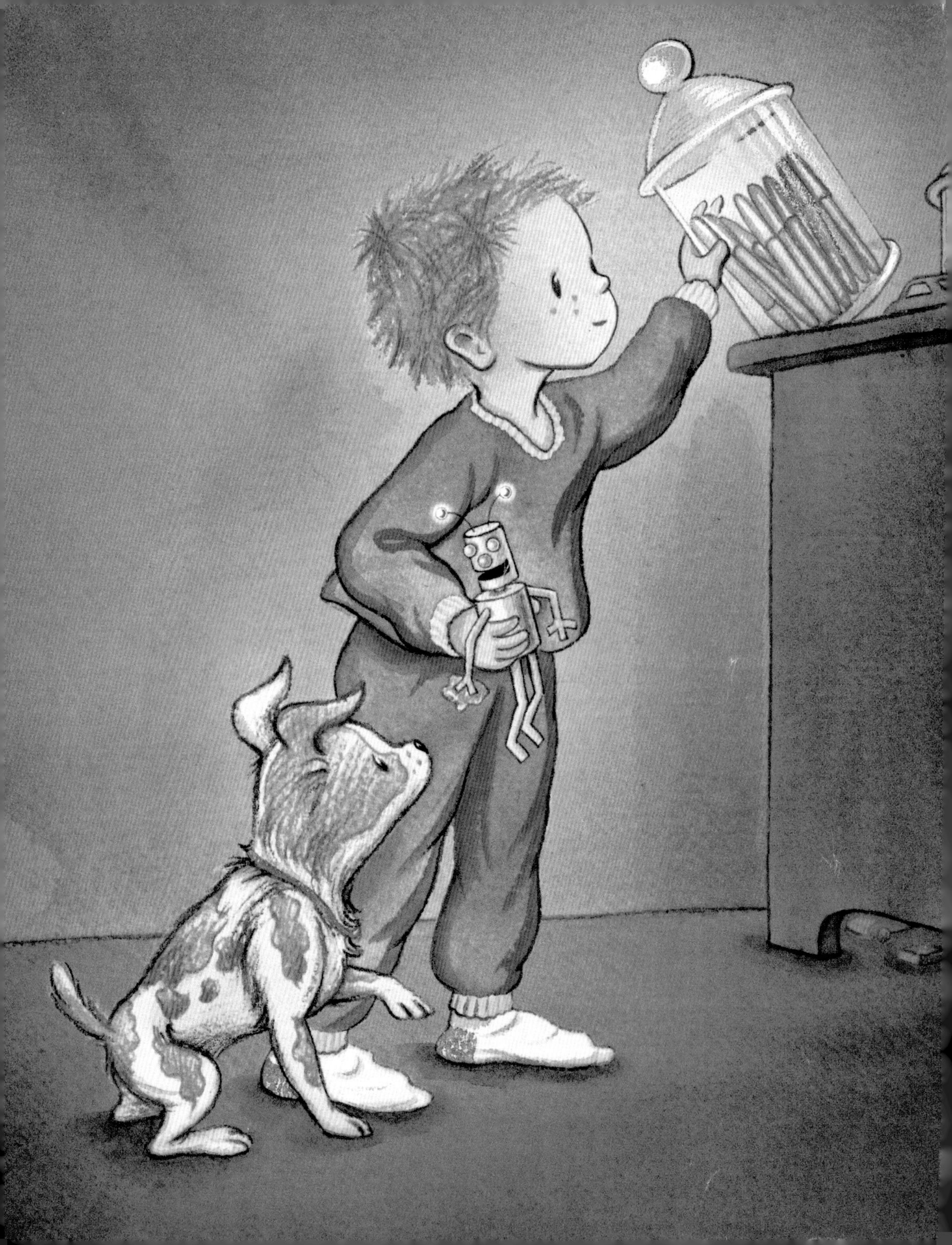

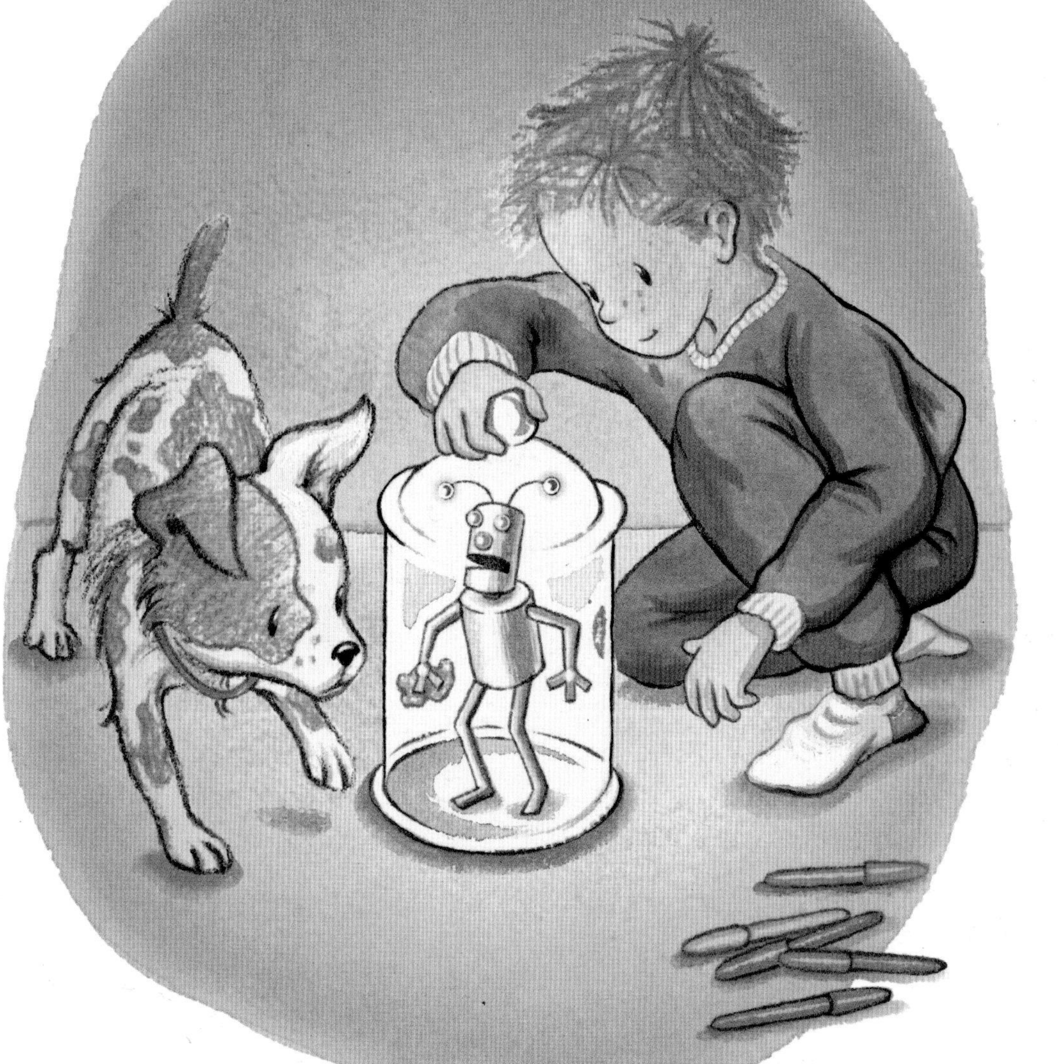

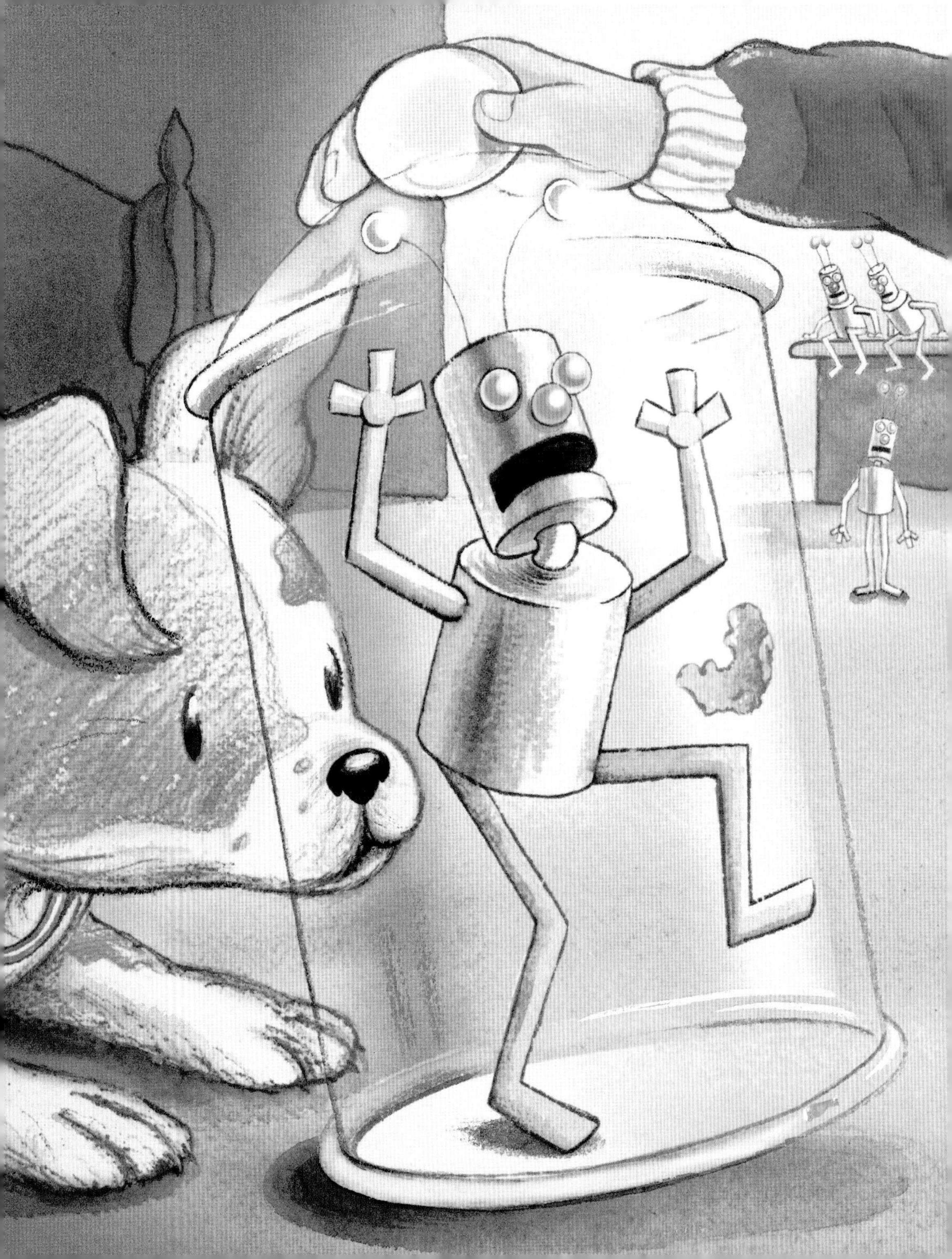

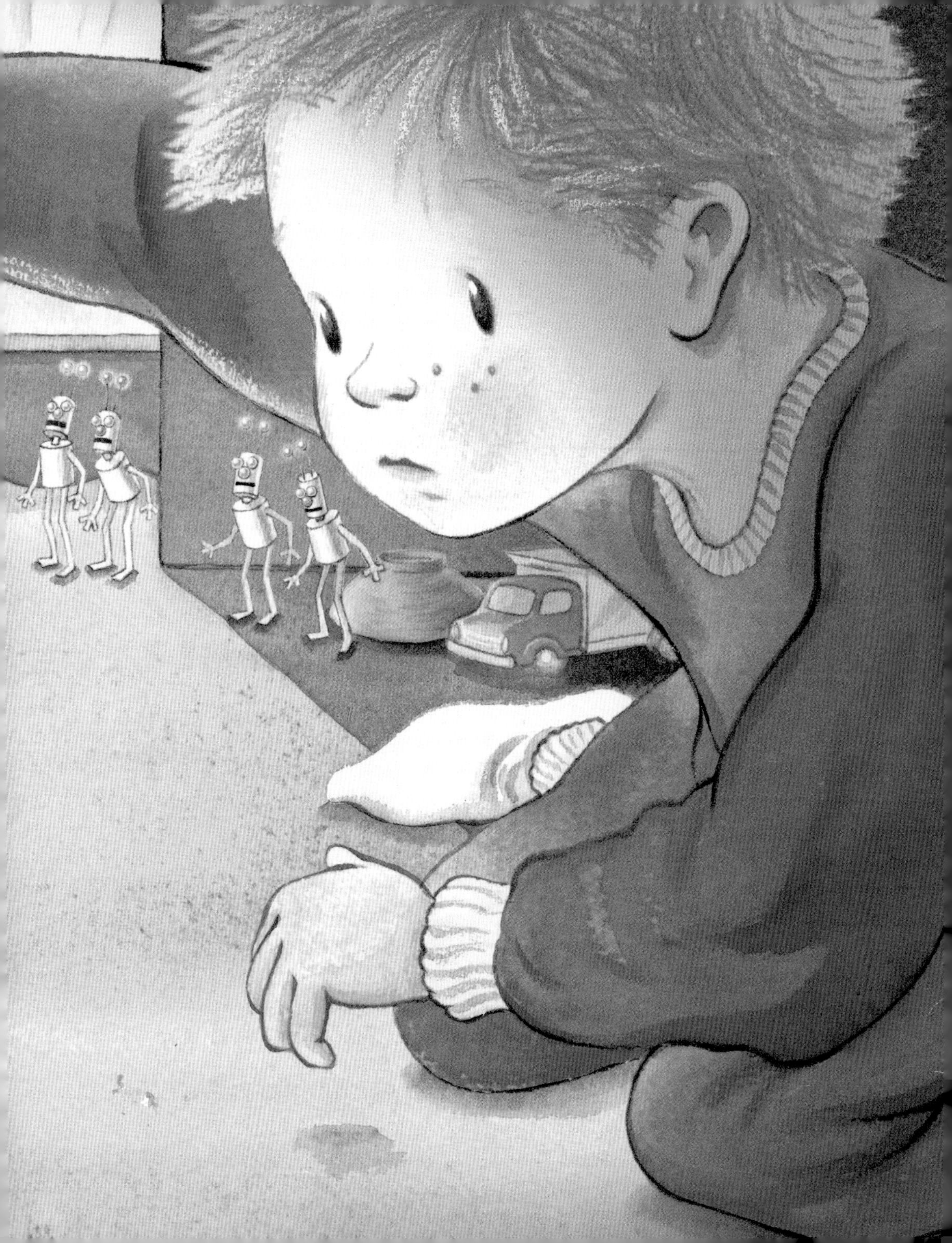

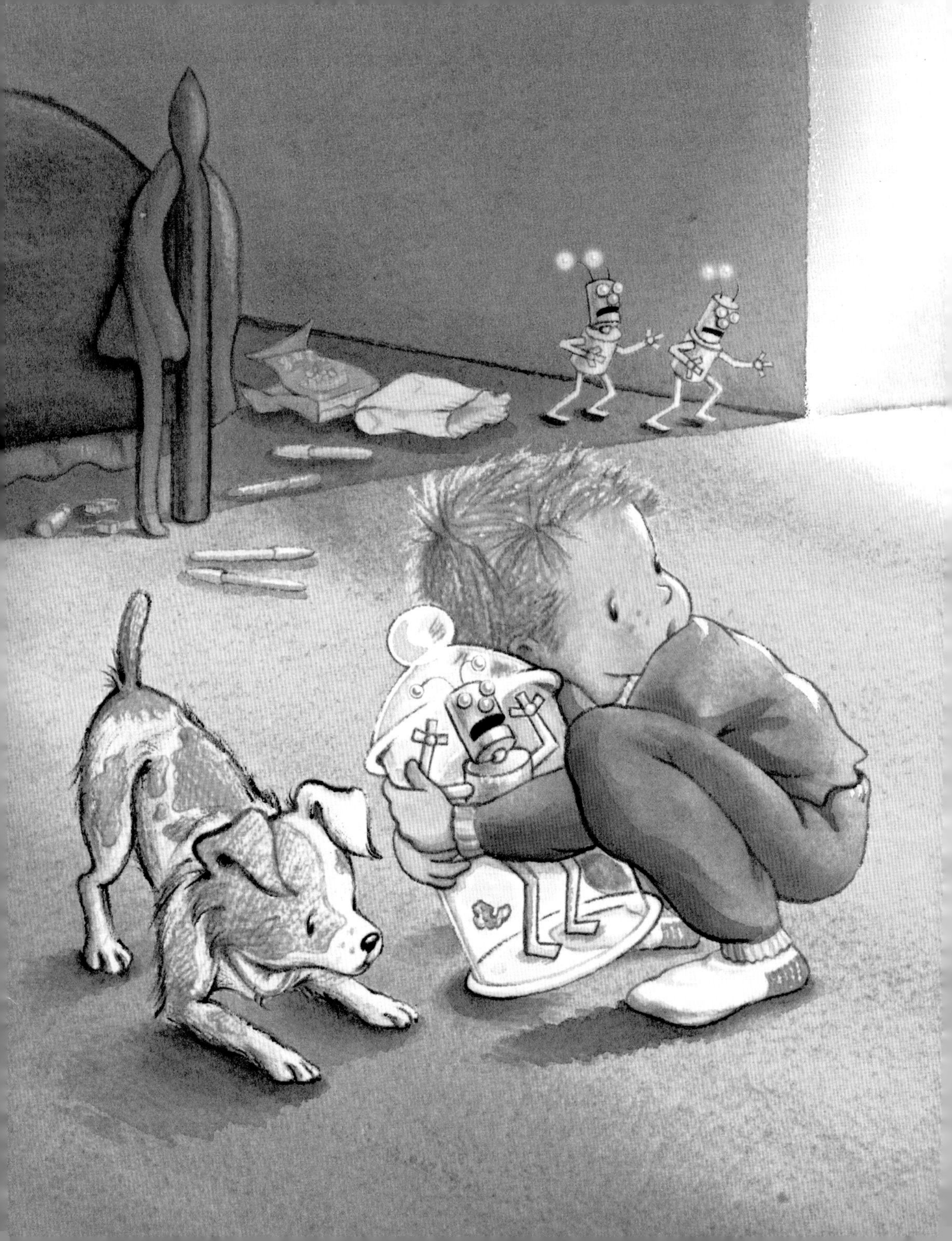

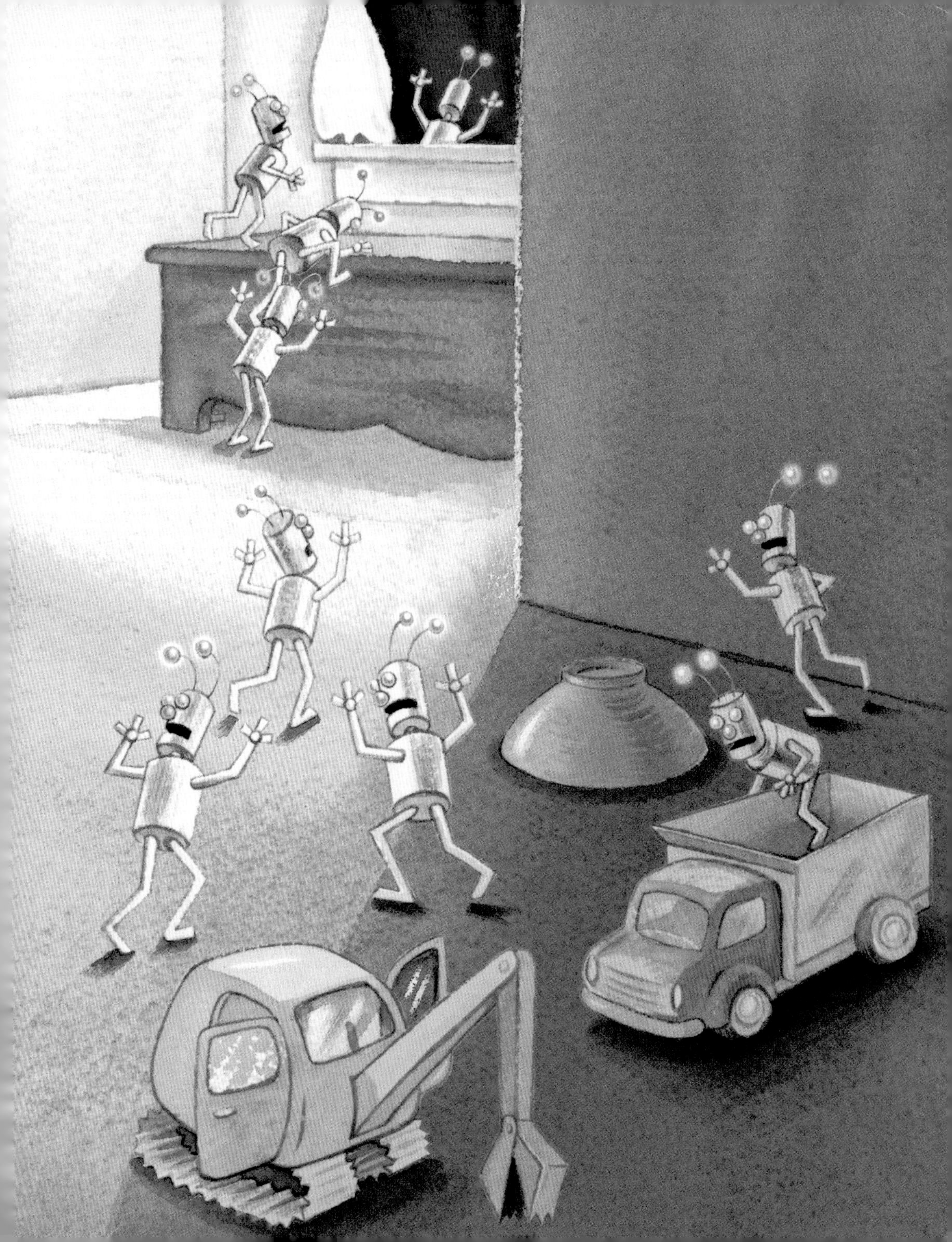

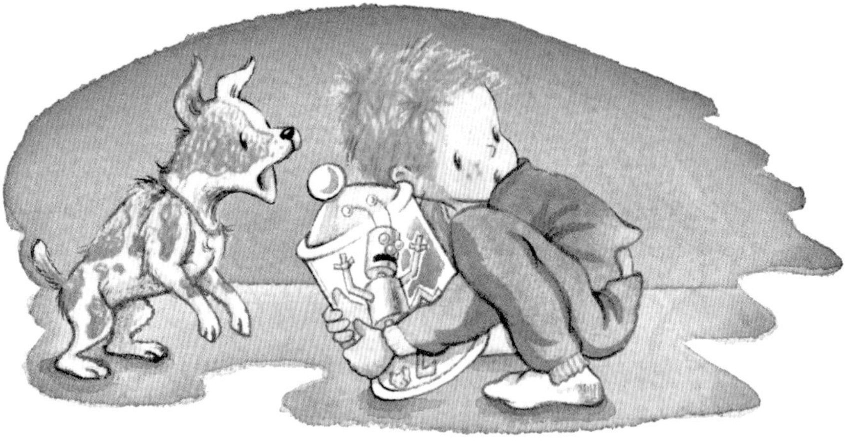

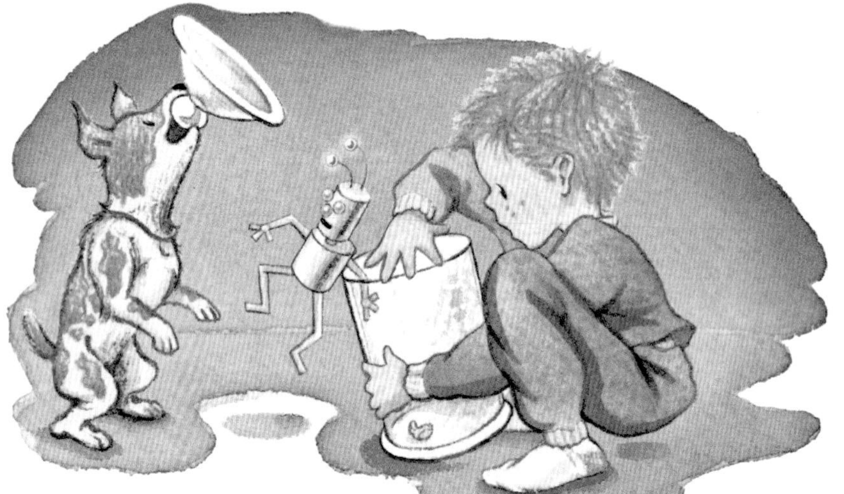

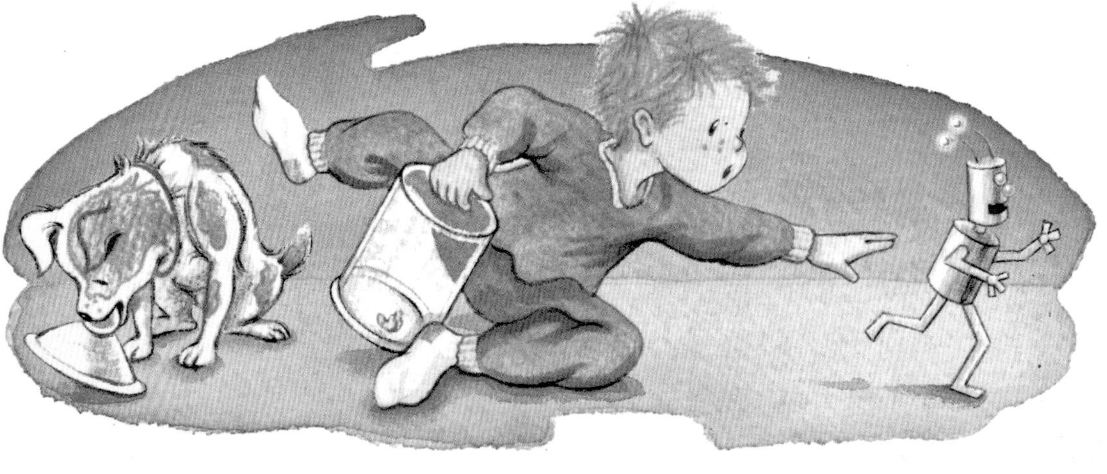

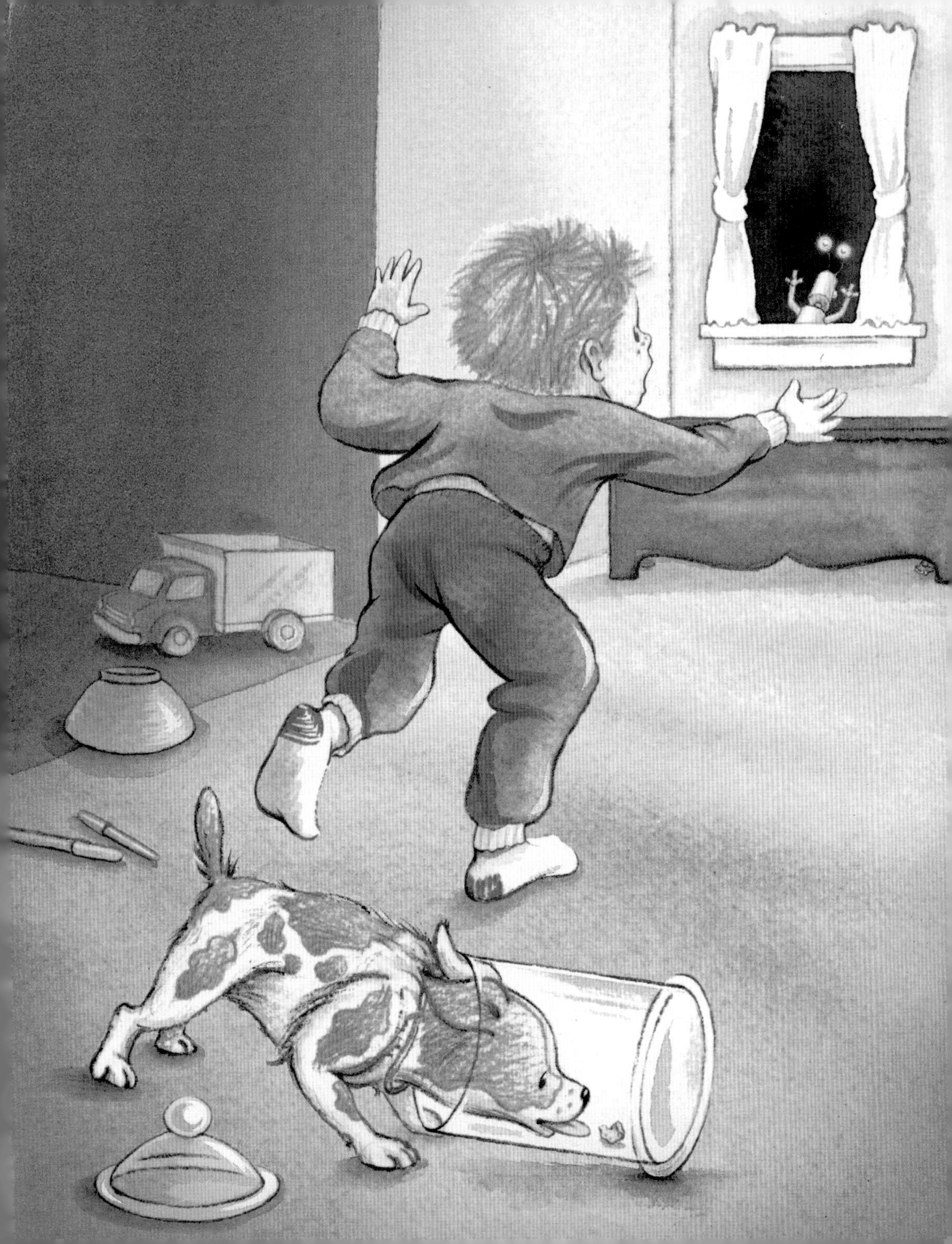

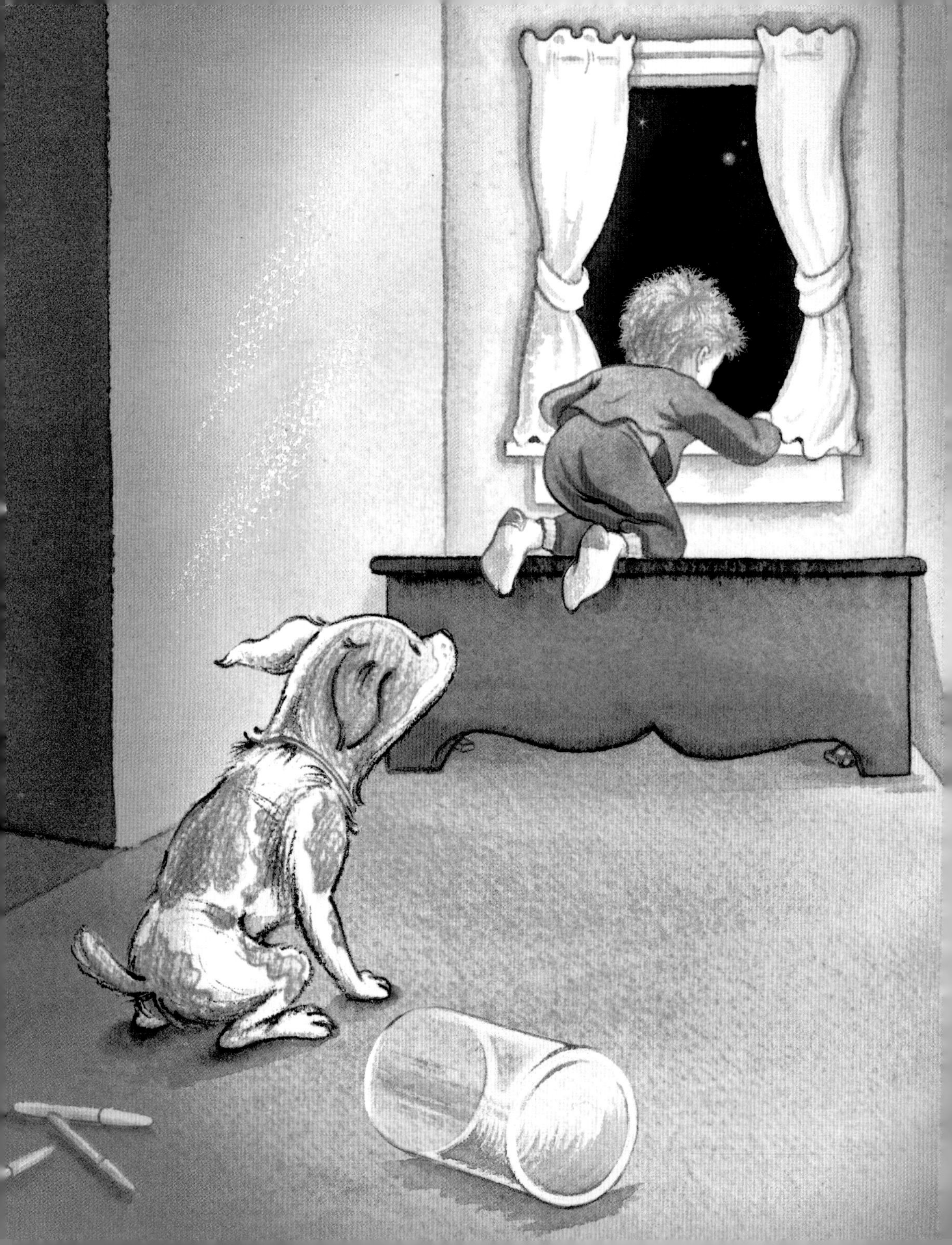

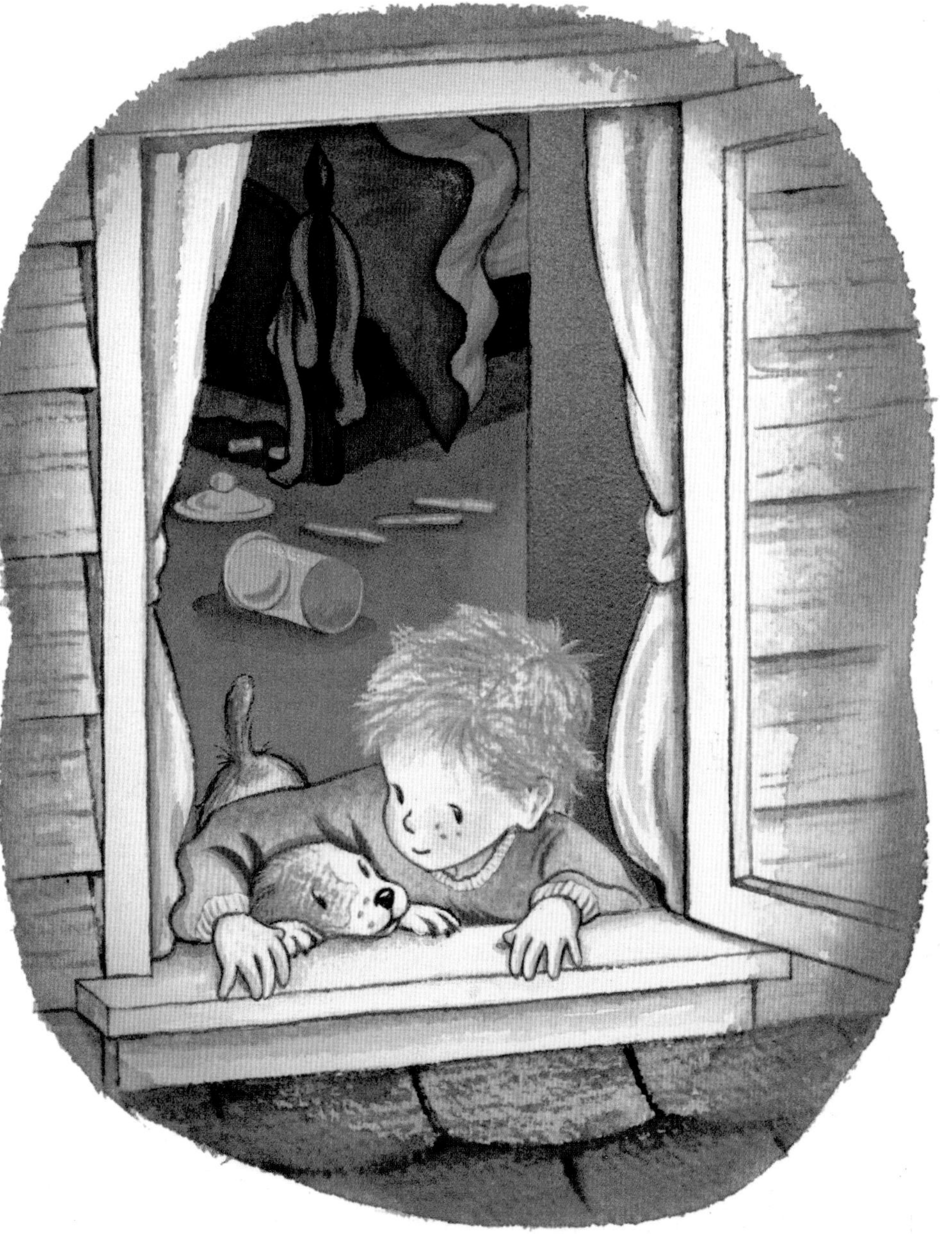